Simon F
Horrid Henry's

Sports Day

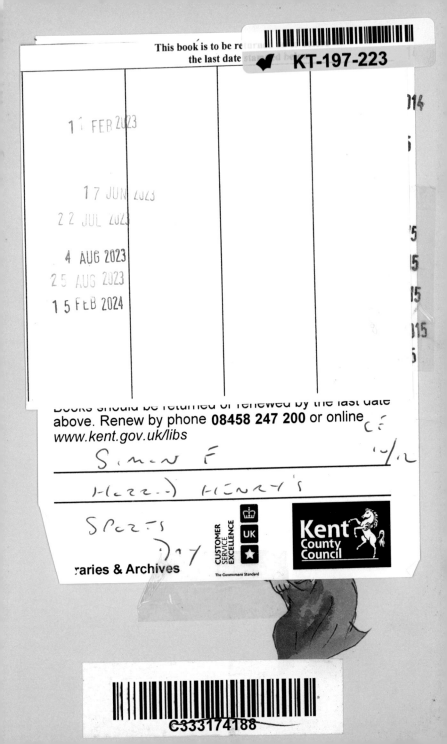

raries & Archives

Kent
County
Council

HORRiD HENRY'S
Sports Day

HORRiD HENRY'S
Sports Day

Francesca Simon
Illustrated by Tony Ross

Orion
Children's Books

Horrid Henry's Sports Day originally appeared in
Horrid Henry Gets Rich Quick first published in
Great Britain in 2002 by Orion Children's Books
This edition first published in Great Britain in 2012
by Orion Children's Books
a division of the Orion Publishing Group Ltd
Orion House
5 Upper Saint Martin's Lane
London WC2H 9EA
An Hachette UK Company

1 3 5 7 9 10 8 6 4 2

A catalogue record for this book is available from the British Library.

ISBN 978 1 4440 0116 7

Printed and bound in China.

www.orionbooks.co.uk
www.horridhenry.co.uk

For Max and Zoë Cutner,
always first past the post.

Look out for . . .

Don't Be Horrid, Henry!
Horrid Henry's Birthday Party
Horrid Henry's Holiday
Horrid Henry's Underpants
Horrid Henry Gets Rich Quick
Horrid Henry and the Football Fiend
Horrid Henry's Nits
Horrid Henry and Moody Margaret
Horrid Henry's Thank You Letter
Horrid Henry Reads A Book
Horrid Henry's Car Journey
Moody Margaret's School
Horrid Henry Tricks and Treats
Horrid Henry's Christmas Play
Horrid Henry's Rainy Day
Horrid Henry's Author Visit
Horrid Henry Meets the Queen

There are many more **Horrid Henry** books
available. For a complete list visit
www.horridhenry.co.uk

or

www.orionbooks.co.uk

Contents

Chapter 1

"We all want Sports Day to be a great success tomorrow," announced Miss Battle-Axe. "I am here to make sure that *no one*" – she glared at Horrid Henry – "spoils it."

Horrid Henry glared back.
Horrid Henry hated Sports Day.
Last year he hadn't won a
single event.

He'd dropped his egg in the
egg-and-spoon race,

tripped over Rude Ralph in the
three-legged race,

and collided with Sour Susan
in the sack race.

Henry's team had even lost
the tug-of-war.

Most sickening of all, Perfect Peter
had won both his races.

If only the school had a sensible day,
like TV-watching day, or chocolate-
eating day, or who could guzzle the
most crisps day, Horrid Henry would
be sure to win every prize.

But no. *He* had to leap and dash about getting hot and bothered in front of stupid parents.

When he became king he'd make teachers run all the races then behead the winners. King Henry the Horrible grinned happily.

"Pay attention, Henry!" barked Miss
Battle-Axe. "What did I just say?"

Henry had no idea.
"Sports Day is cancelled?"
he suggested hopefully.

Miss Battle-Axe fixed him with her steely eyes. "I said no one is to bring any sweets tomorrow. You'll all be given a delicious, refreshing piece of orange."

Henry slumped in his chair, scowling. All he could do was hope for rain.

Chapter 2

Sports Day dawned bright and sunny.

Rats, thought Henry.
He could, of course, pretend to
be sick. But he'd tried that last year
and Mum hadn't been fooled.

The year before that he'd complained he'd hurt his leg. Unfortunately Dad then caught him dancing on the table.

It was no use. He'd just have to take part. If only he could win a race!

Perfect Peter bounced into his room.
"Sports Day today!" beamed Peter.
"And *I'm* responsible for bringing
the hard-boiled eggs for the egg-and-
spoon race. Isn't it exciting!"

"NO!" screeched Henry.
"Get out of here!"

"But I only…" began Peter.

Henry leapt at him, roaring. He was
a cowboy lassoing a runaway steer.
"Eeeaaargh!" squealed Peter.

"Stop being horrid, Henry!"
shouted Dad.
"Or no pocket money this week!"
Henry let Peter go.

"It's so unfair," he muttered, picking up his clothes from the floor and putting them on.
Why did he never win?

Chapter 3

Henry reached under his bed and filled his pockets from the secret sweet tin he kept there.

Horrid Henry was a master at eating
sweets in school without being
detected. At least he could scoff
something good while the others
were stuck eating dried-up old
orange pieces.

Then he stomped downstairs.

Perfect Peter was busy packing
hard-boiled eggs into a carton.
Horrid Henry sat down scowling
and gobbled his breakfast.

"Good luck, boys," said Mum.
"I'll be there to cheer for you."

"Humph," growled Henry.

"Thanks, Mum," said Peter.
"I expect I'll win my egg-and-spoon
race again but of course it doesn't
matter if I don't. It's how you play
that counts."

"Shut up, Peter!" snarled Henry.

Egg-and-spoon!

Egg-and-spoon!

If Henry heard that disgusting phrase
once more he would start frothing
at the mouth.

"Mum! Henry told me to shut up," wailed Peter, "and he attacked me this morning."

"Stop being horrid, Henry," said Mum. "Peter, come with me and we'll comb your hair. I want you to look your best when you win that trophy again."

Henry's blood boiled. He felt like snatching those eggs and hurling them against the wall.

Then Henry had a wonderful,
spectacular idea. It was so
wonderful that… Henry heard Mum
coming back down the stairs.
There was no time to lose crowing
about his brilliance.

Horrid Henry ran to the fridge,
grabbed another egg carton and
swapped it for the box of hard-boiled
ones on the counter.

"Don't forget your eggs, Peter," said Mum. She handed the carton to Peter, who tucked it safely in his school bag.

Tee hee, thought Horrid Henry.

Chapter 4

Henry's class lined up on the
playing fields.

Flash!

A small figure wearing gleaming
white trainers zipped by.
It was Aerobic Al, the fastest boy
in Henry's class.

"Gotta run, gotta run, gotta run,"
he chanted, gliding into place beside
Henry. "I will, of course, win every
event," he announced.
"I've been training all year.
My dad's got a special place all ready
for my trophies."

"Who wants to race anyway?"
sneered Horrid Henry, sneaking
a yummy gummy fuzzball into
his mouth.

"Now, teams for the three-legged race," barked Miss Battle-Axe into her megaphone. "This is a race showing how well you co-operate and use teamwork with your partner.

Ralph will race with William,

Josh will race with Clare,

Henry…" She glanced at her list.
"You will race with Margaret."

"NO!"

screamed Horrid Henry.

"NO!"

screamed Moody Margaret.

"Yes," said Miss Battle-Axe.

"But I want to be with Susan," said Margaret.

"No fussing," said Miss Battle-Axe.
"Bert, where's your partner?"

"I dunno," said Beefy Bert.

Henry and Margaret stood as far apart as possible while their legs were tied together.

"You'd better do as I say, Henry," hissed Margaret.
"*I'll* decide how we race."

"*I* will, you mean," hissed Henry.

"Ready … steady …GO!"
Miss Battle-Axe blew her whistle.
They were off!

Chapter 5

Henry moved to the left,
Margaret moved to the right.

"This way, Henry!" shouted
Margaret. She tried to drag him.

"No, this way!" shouted Henry.
He tried to drag her.

They lurched wildly, left and right,
then toppled over.

CRASH!

Aerobic Al and Lazy Linda
tripped over the screaming Henry
and Margaret.

SMASH!

Rude Ralph and Weepy William
fell over Al and Linda.

BUMP!

Dizzy Dave and Beefy Bert collided
with Ralph and William.

"Waaa!"
wailed Weepy William.

"It's all your fault, Margaret!"
shouted Henry, pulling her hair.

"No, yours," shouted Margaret,
pulling his harder.

Miss Battle-Axe blew her whistle
frantically.

"Stop! Stop!" she ordered.
"Henry! Margaret! What an example
to set for the younger ones.
Any more nonsense like that and
you'll be severely punished.

Everyone, get ready for the egg-and-spoon race!"

This was it!
The moment Henry had been waiting for.

The children lined up in their teams.
Moody Margaret, Sour Susan and
Anxious Andrew were going first
in Henry's class.

Henry glanced at Peter.
Yes, there he was, smiling proudly,
next to Goody-Goody Gordon,
Spotless Sam, and Tidy Ted.
The eggs lay still on their spoons.

Horrid Henry held his breath.

"Ready ... steady ... GO!"
shouted Miss Battle-Axe.

They were off!

Chapter 6

"Go, Peter, go!" shouted Mum.

Peter walked faster
and faster and faster.

He was in the lead.
He was pulling away from the field.

Then ...

w_obble ...

w_obble ...

SPLAT!

"Aaaaagh!" yelped Peter.

Moody Margaret's egg wobbled.

SPLAT!

 Then Susan's.

SPLAT!

Then everybody's.

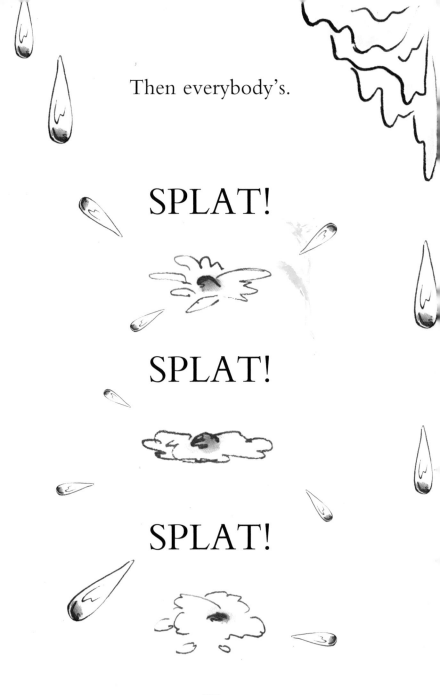

SPLAT!

SPLAT!

SPLAT!

"I've got egg on my shoes!"
wailed Margaret.

"I've ruined my new dress!"
shrieked Susan.

"I've got egg all over me!"
squealed Tidy Ted.

"Help!" squeaked Perfect Peter.
Egg dripped down his trousers.

Parents surged forward,
screaming and waving
handkerchiefs and towels.

Rude Ralph and Horrid Henry
shrieked with laughter.

Miss Battle-Axe blew her whistle.
"Who brought the eggs?" asked Miss
Battle-Axe. Her voice was like ice.

"I did," said Perfect Peter.
"But I brought hard-boiled ones."

"OUT!" shouted Miss Battle-Axe.
"Out of the games!"

"But … but …" gasped
Perfect Peter.

"No buts, out!" she glared.
"Go straight to the Head."

Perfect Peter burst into tears
and crept away.

Horrid Henry could hardly contain himself. This was the best Sports Day he'd ever been to.

"The rest of you stop laughing at
once. Parents, get back to your seats!
Time for the next race!"
ordered Miss Battle-Axe.

Chapter 7

All things considered, thought Horrid Henry, lining up with his class, it hadn't been too terrible a day.

He'd loved the egg-and-spoon race, of course. And he'd had fun pulling the other team into a muddy puddle in the tug-of-war, knocking over the obstacles in the obstacle race, and crashing into Aerobic Al in the sack race.

But, oh, to actually win something!

There was just one race left before Sports Day was over. The cross-country run. The event Henry hated more than any other. One long, sweaty, exhausting lap round the whole field.

Henry heaved his heavy bones to the
starting line. His final chance to win
… yet he knew there was no hope.
If he beat Weepy William
he'd be doing well.

Suddenly Henry had a wonderful,
spectacular idea. Why had he never
thought of this before?
Truly, he was a genius.

Wasn't there some ancient Greek who'd won a race by throwing down golden apples which his rival kept stopping to pick up?

Couldn't he, Henry, learn something from those old Greeks?

"Ready …steady … GO!"
shrieked Miss Battle-Axe.

Off they dashed.

"Go, Al, go!" yelled his father.

"Do your best, Henry," said Mum.

Horrid Henry reached into his
pocket and hurled some sweets.
They thudded to the ground
in front of the runners.

"Look, sweets!" shouted Henry.

Al checked behind him.
He was well in the lead. He paused
and scooped up one sweet, and then
another. He glanced behind again,
then started unwrapping the yummy
gummy fuzzball.

"Sweets!" yelped Greedy Graham.
He stopped to pick up as many
as he could find then stuffed them
in his mouth.
"Yummy!" screamed Graham.

"Sweets! Where?" chanted the others. Then they stopped to look.

"Over there!" yelled Henry, throwing another handful.

The racers paused to pounce on the treats.

While the others munched and crunched, Henry made a frantic dash for the lead.

 He was out in front!

Henry's legs moved as they had never moved before, pounding round the field. And there was the finishing line!

  THUD!

 THUD!

 THUD!

Henry glanced back.
Oh no! Aerobic Al was catching up!

Henry felt in his pocket. He had one
giant gob-stopper left. He looked
round, panting.

"Go home and take a nap, Henry!"
shouted Al, sticking out his tongue
as he raced past.

Henry threw down the gob-stopper
in front of Al. Aerobic Al hesitated,
then skidded to a halt and picked it
up. He could beat Henry any day so
why not show off a bit?

Suddenly Henry sprinted past.
Aerobic Al dashed after him.
Harder and harder, faster and faster
Henry ran. He was a bird.
He was a plane.
He flew across the finishing line.

"The winner is … Henry?"
squeaked Miss Battle-Axe.

"I've been robbed!"
screamed Aerobic Al.

"Hurray!" yelled Henry.

Wow, what a great day, thought
Horrid Henry, proudly carrying
home his trophy. Al's dad shouting
at Miss Battle-Axe. Miss Battle-Axe
and Mum shouting back.
Peter sent off in disgrace.
And he, Henry, the big winner.

"I can't think how you got those eggs muddled up," said Mum.

"Me neither," said Perfect Peter, sniffling.

"Never mind, Peter," said Henry brightly. "It's not winning, it's *how* you play that counts."